Fun in the Sun

BY MARV ALINAS · ILLUSTRATED BY KATHLEEN PETELINSEK

Today I am going to have some **fun**.
I will go play in the **sun**!

My dad jokes. He makes a **pun**.
I smile. My dad likes to have **fun**.

I go outside. I start to **run**.
I like to **run** in the warm **sun**.

Where should I **run**?

I **run** past the bakery. I see a **bun**.
The **bun** is sitting in the **sun**.

I go inside. I buy the **bun**.
Eating the **bun** will be **fun**!

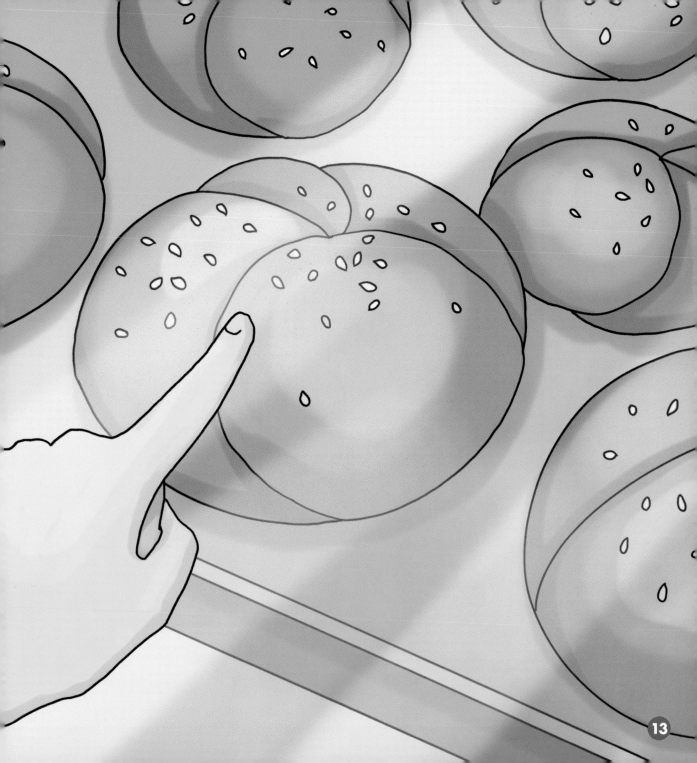

I run with my **bun**.

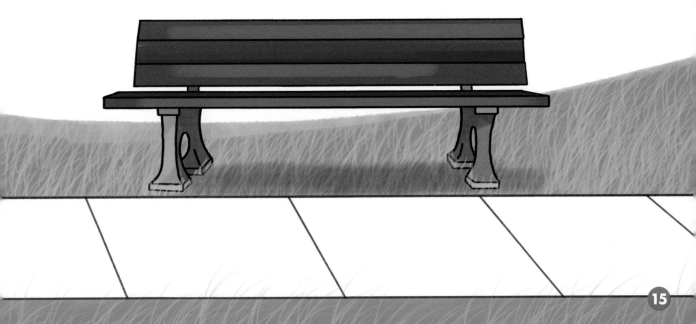

Now it is time to eat my **bun**.
I will eat my **bun** in the warm **sun**.

Now where should I **run**?

I **run** home in the warm **sun**.
It is **fun** to **run** in the **sun**!

Word List

bun   run

fun   sun

pun

Which Words Rhyme?

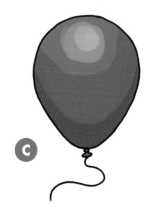

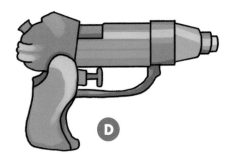

About the Author

Marv Alinas has written dozens of books for children. When she's not reading or writing, Marv enjoys spending time with her husband and dogs and traveling to interesting places. Marv lives in Minnesota.

About the Illustrator

Kathleen Petelinsek has loved to draw since she was a child. Through the years, she has designed and illustrated hundreds of books for kids. She lives in Minnesota with her husband, two dogs, and new kitten.

The Child's World
childsworld.com

Published by The Child's World®
1980 Lookout Drive • Mankato, MN 56003-1705
800-599-READ • www.childsworld.com

ISBN: 9781503823594
LCCN: 2017944772

Printed in the United States of America
PA02391